Flip and Flop Celebrate Family!

by Janis Ingham

Illustrator: Sue Durham

AuthorHouse™
1663 Liberty Drive, Suite 200
Bloomington, IN 47403
www.authorhouse.com
Phone: 1-800-839-8640

First published by AuthorHouse   1/27/2009

ISBN: 978-1-4389-2152-5 (sc)

Printed in the United States of America
Bloomington, Indiana

This book is printed on acid-free paper.

authorHOUSE®

Flip and Flop Celebrate Family!

Flip and Flop are very close.

They share a Mom and Dad who call them "the twins".

They are part of something cool called a family and that is where this book begins.

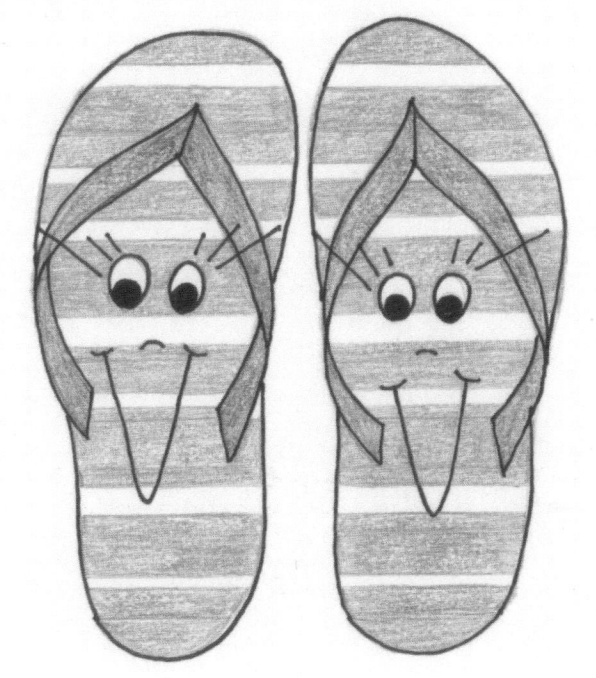

Flip and Flop were wondering ...

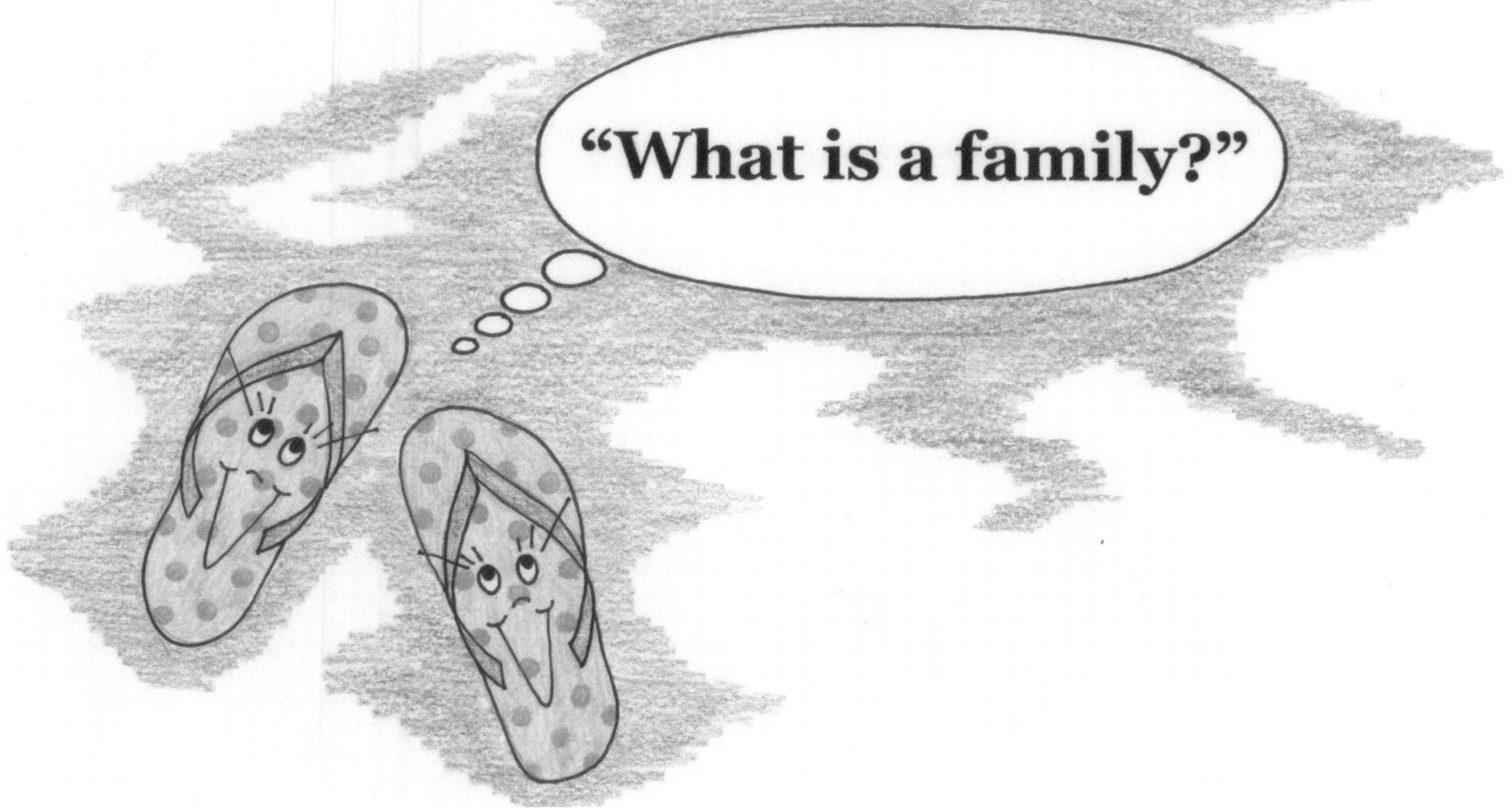

Flip and Flop thought long and hard.

They thought about who they loved and why.

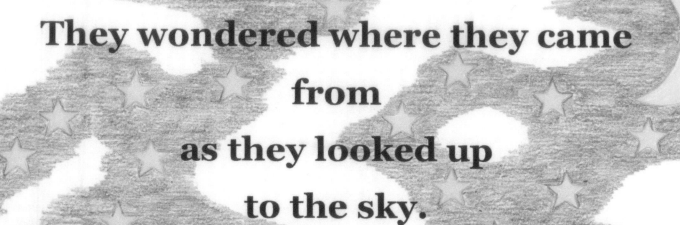

They wondered where they came
from
as they looked up
to the sky.

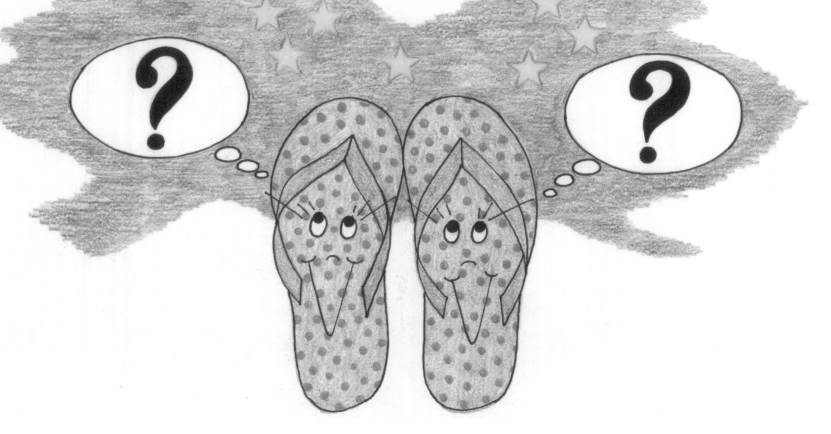

Flip and Flop did lots of soul searching and talked to every friend around.

They wrote down everything they heard, and here is what they found.

?

how

where

what

who

when

why

A family is a mom, a dad, and kids ~ lots of times that's true.

But over the years things have changed, and Flip and Flop wanted to explore

what's

new.

So many different kinds of families.
Some live together. Some do not.

Some have two parents and lots of kids.
Others have one parent and maybe just one
tot.

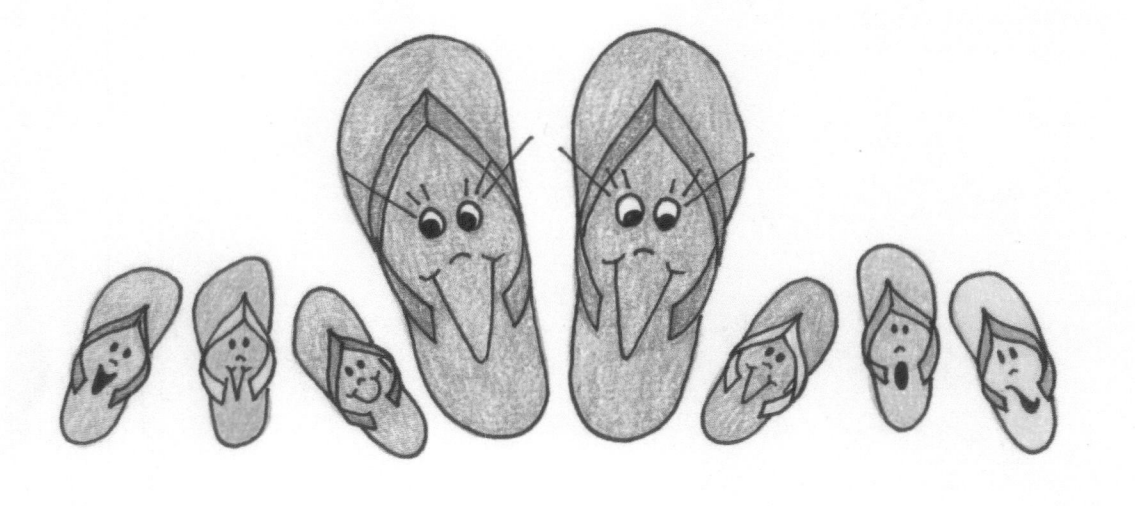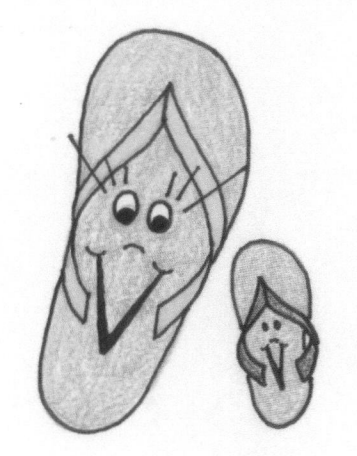

Grandparents often get involved.
Adoptions are also cool.

Families all seem to be unique-
a group that cares is the
general rule.

Families come in many forms.

Some are **big** and some are small.

Flip and Flop believe that whatever family you are in

is

the

most special

one

of

all!!

Families provide lots of things.
They provide shelter from a storm.
They provide clothing and comfort and most
importantly ~
LOVE
to
keep
you
warm.

Families meet so many needs
that others can't provide.

Flip and Flop say be thankful to
have your family by your side.

Family members have many jobs, lots of responsibilities and chores to do.

Families work together like Flip and Flop ~ like me and you.

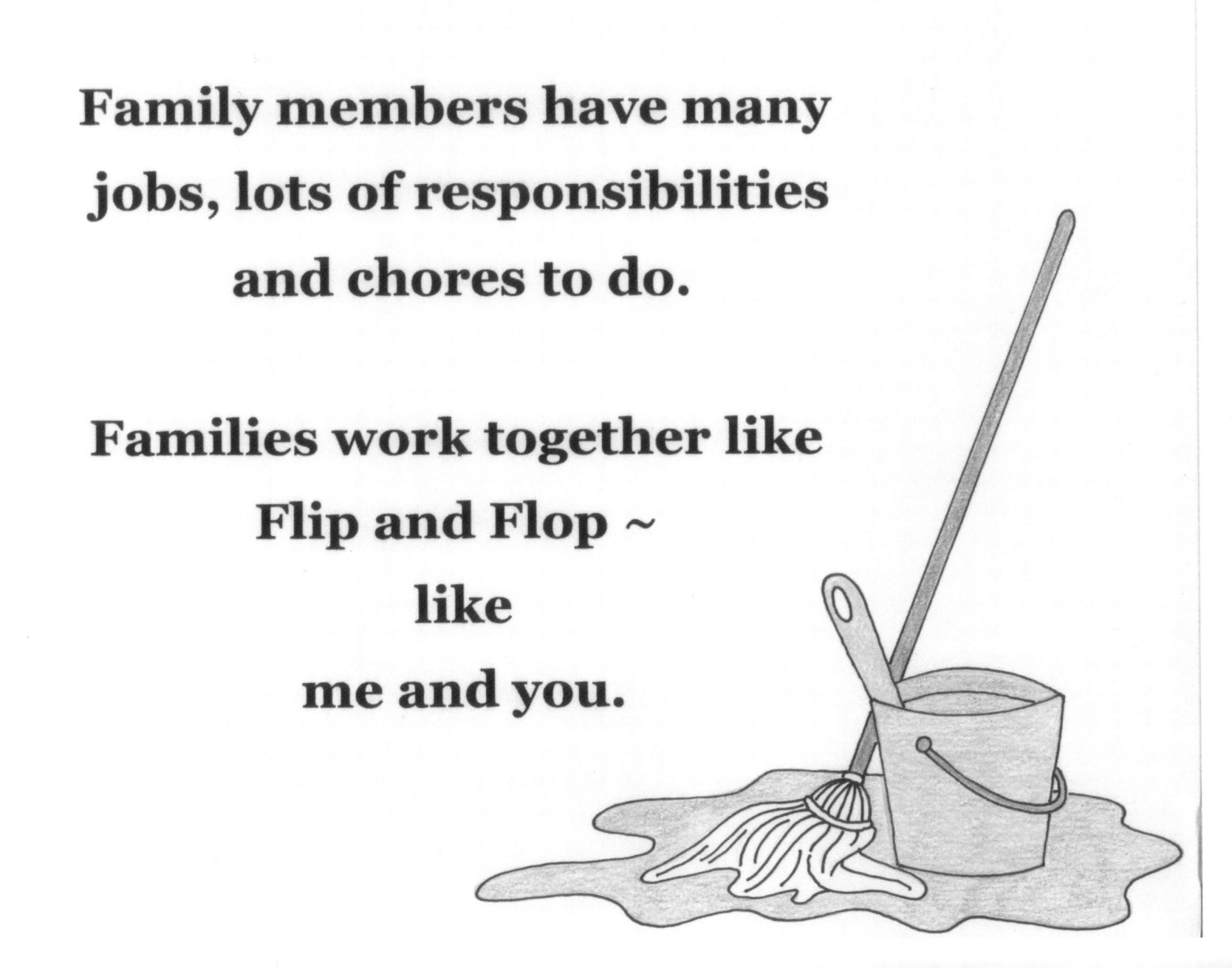

All families have a history.

Flip and Flop wondered what theirs would be.

They did a lot of research
and they created a family tree.

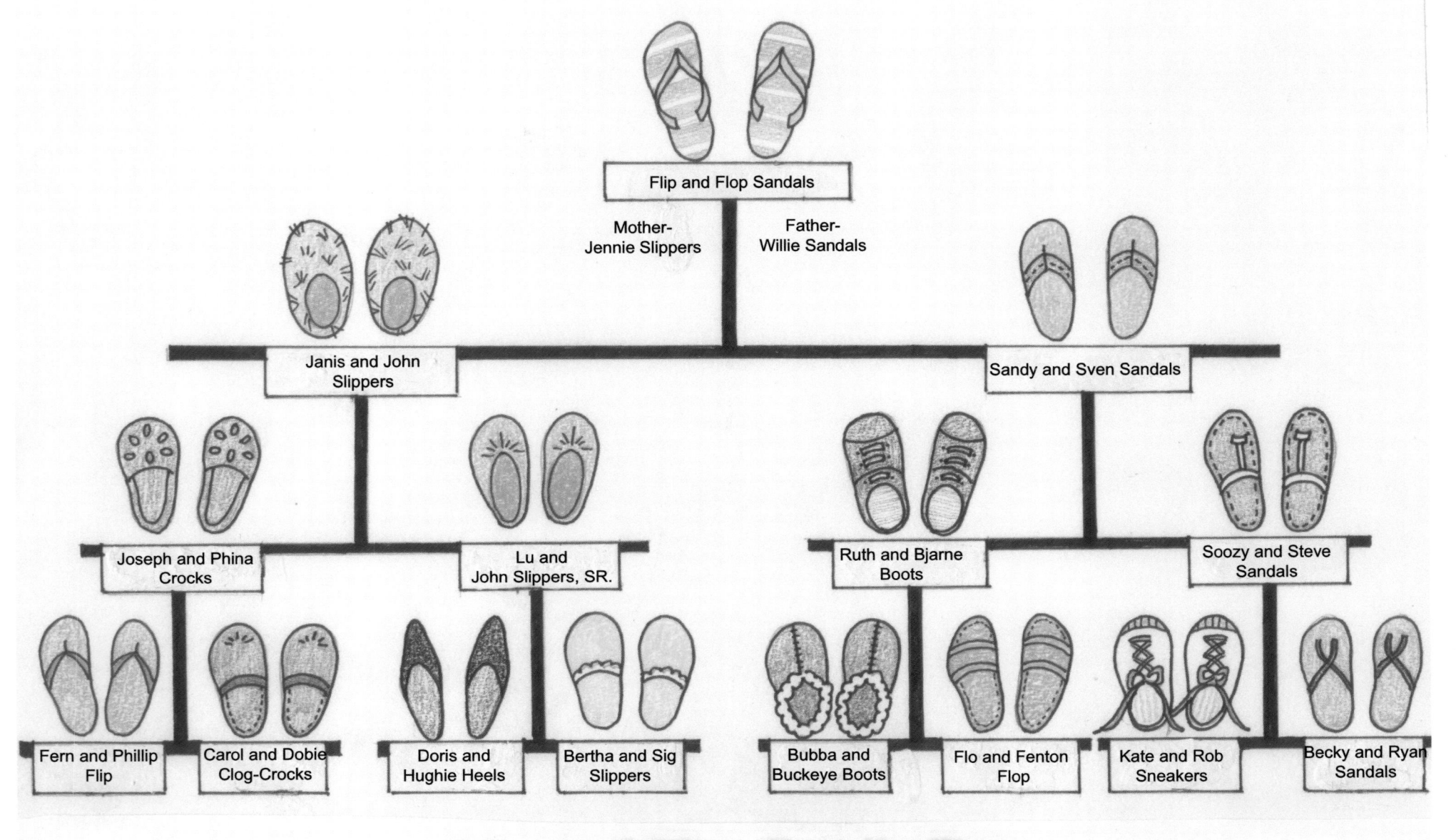

Flip and Flop Family Tree

(Four Generations)

Flip and Flop discovered their family history.

They learned about their roots.

They learned about
Grandma Sandy Sandals
and
Great Grandpa Bjarne Boots.

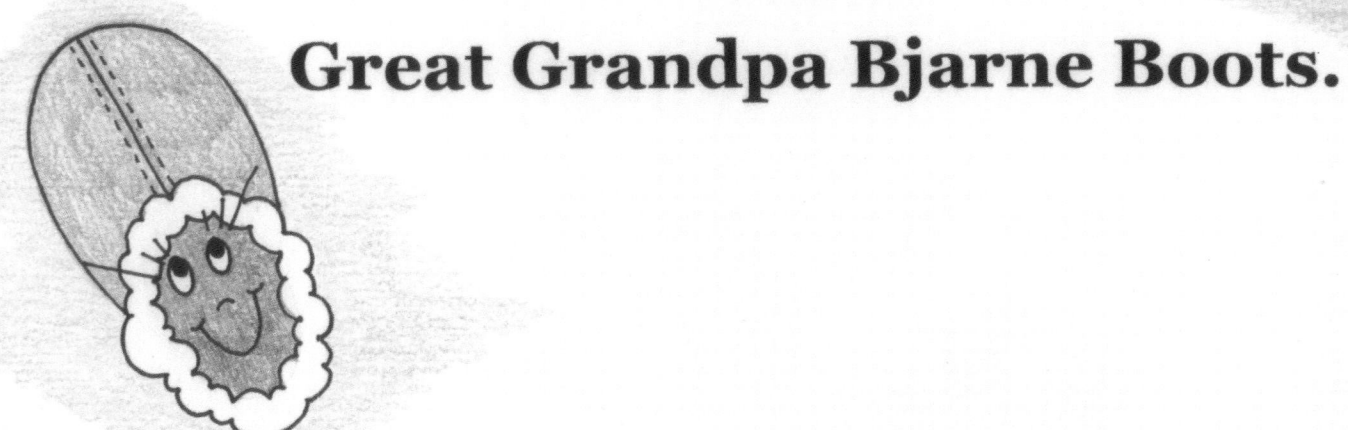

They found out they were named for
Great-Great Grandparents
Fenton Flop
and
Phillip Flip!

They learned that in the 70's, Great-Great Grandparents Bubba and Buckeye Boots were really pretty hip!

Family heritage is fun to learn.

It can make you very proud.

Links to the past are special.

They make memories

speak

out

loud!

Family histories are so interesting.
Flip and Flop could go
on and on
about things they found out...

They encourage you to look into your past to
discover your roots
and what your family's all about.

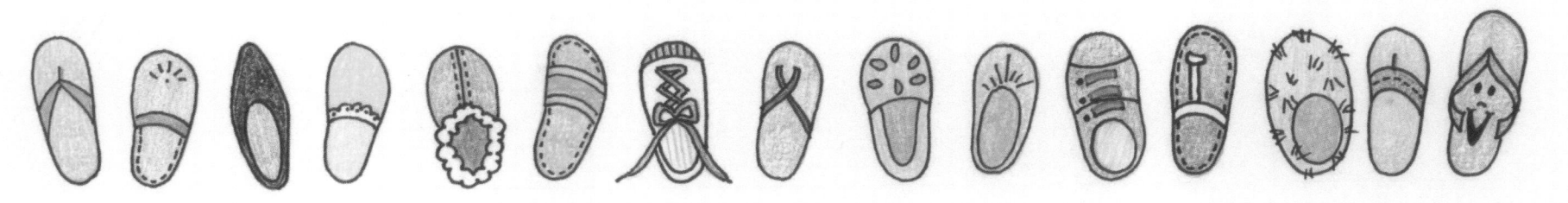

Families give you roots and as you grow they give you wings.

Families give you joy and teach you to love what your life brings.

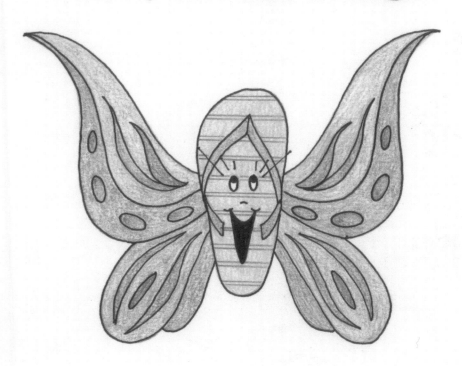

Each family is special.
Accept and love yours as they are.

Remember, family is the most

important part of your

<u>whole</u>

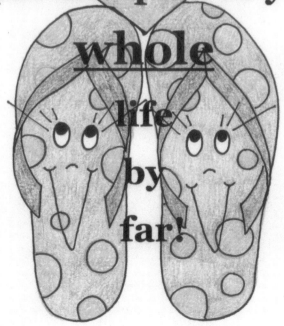

life

by

far!

Celebrate YOUR family!

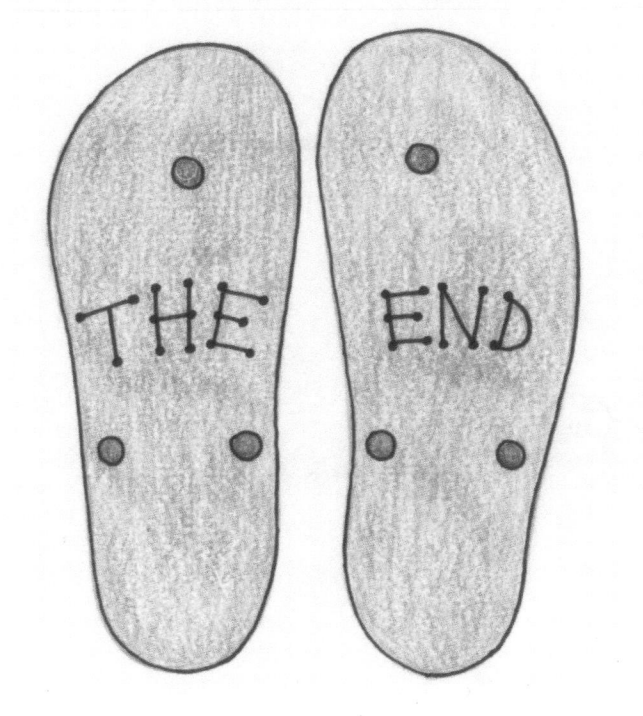

Create your own Family Tree!

See how far back you can trace your family history.

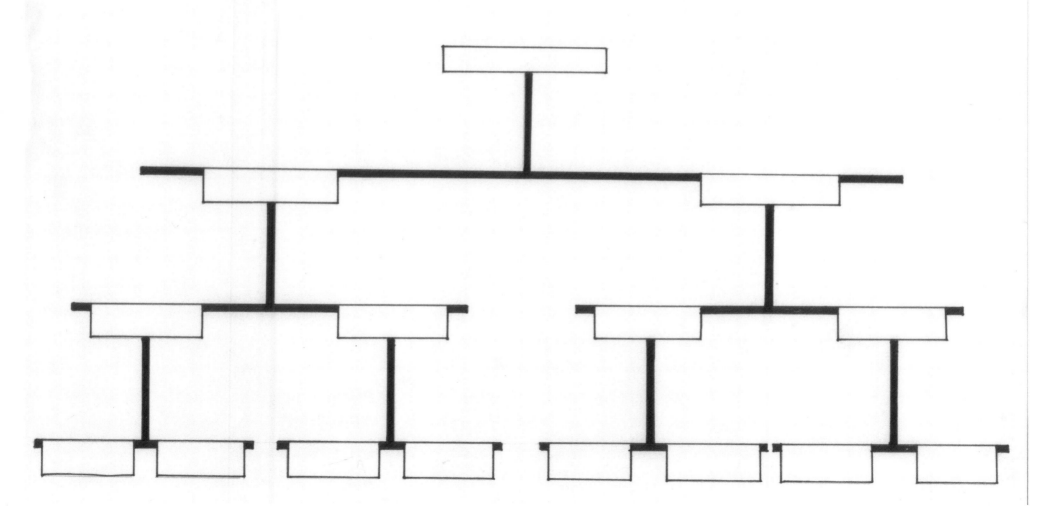